# Plants make friends too

# Plants make friends too

Sukanya Datta

wisdom tree

First published 2008; Reprint January 2012



ISBN 13: 978-81-8328-025-9

*Published by*
Wisdom Tree
4779/23 Ansari Road
Darya Ganj
New Delhi-110002
*Ph.*: 23247966/67/68

*Published by* Shobit Arya for Wisdom Tree; *edited by* Manju Gupta; *designed by* Priya Nagarajan and Joanna Mendes; *typeset at* Marks & Strokes, New Delhi-110002 and *printed in* India.

*This book is dedicated to my beloved* 'Boro-mami', *Mrs Geeta Datta, who is grace personified and dignity incarnate. In amazing appreciation of her capacity to knit the family together with love.*

This book is dedicated to my beloved 'Boro-mami', Mrs Geeta Datta, who is grace personified and dignity incarnate. In amazing appreciation of her capacity to knit the family together with love.

# Contents

# Preface

Everybody needs friends. We make friends usually with those we meet often. Many of our classmates become our friends. We stay in touch even after school and sometimes visit each other's home. Those who live nearby too become friends. We seek them out to chat or to play or simply be with. We may even make friends with those who live in another country by writing letters or e-mailing them. Friends make us happy. Friends make life easier. We laugh when we are with friends. Friends help wipe our tears when we are sad. Friends hold our hand and speak up for us when we are in trouble. Friendship is a warm feeling.

Friendship means companionship.

By making friends and learning the art of friendship, we also learn the art of being social. We realise human beings cannot live alone. We depend on one another and live in groups or communities. That is why we say man is a social animal. Ideally it means that all humans need to make friends and live together in harmony. In a harmonious society, every individual supports and helps the other.

The benefits of living and working together are so great that many animals also exhibit social tendencies. The monkey society is structured with a 'boss' at the top whom everybody obeys. It is the boss's duty to ensure that the young males defend the group and extend protection to the females and young ones in case of danger. A wolf pack has a leader too. He is called the 'alpha male'. The others in the pack follow the alpha male so that discipline is maintained. The 'boss' or the alpha male is obeyed without question till he becomes old or weak or for some reason is unable to defend his position at the top. In that case, a brief struggle for power ensues and another individual gets the 'job'. Hens have a pecking order and individuals high up on the pecking scale can peck those below them. But those lower down on the pecking scale never peck those above them! Ant, bee, and termite societies are rigidly structured with each insect having a well-defined role to play while the queen ant or bee performs the central role.

In an ant society the queen ant performs the central role.

If you see pet dogs of different owners in a park, you will notice that they band together in packs in the brief time that they are together. Even humans often treat their pets as valued friends. Many claim that they can understand what their pets want and that their pets in turn, understand them. It does not matter that the pet is an animal and the owner, a human.

Like humans, you will find pet dogs banding together.

But we never seem to include the great plant kingdom when we discuss friendship or even their ability to communicate.

If sociability provides such great advantages, how is it that plants do not seem to need friends at all?

Plants breathe, use food, grow and reproduce. These are all signs of life. Friends are intrinsic to life. So how is it that plants do not seem to need friends? Or is it that we have never observed them closely enough?

The truth is that plants too need friends and make friends as well. It is just that they are not 'vocal' about their needs or show off their ability to make friends. They evolved on Earth long before the animals did. For many years they had the Earth to themselves. So their rules are a little different to those that govern us. The truth is that plants have friends (and enemies) too. It is just that we have never looked deeply enough.

We presume that since plants cannot talk and most cannot move, they are unable to express their needs. We think that plants have no needs except that they require sunlight, soil and water. But a gardener who spends long hours with plants will tell us that plants send out subtle signals regarding what they want. A wilted plant is thirsty. Wilting is the signal that makes a gardener rush for the sprinkler or watering can! Withering or discolouration of leaf margins indicates nutritional deficiencies. All good gardeners have learnt to understand this and other signals. But gardeners are not the only friends that plants have.

A gardener who is devoted to his plants, tells us that plants respond by sending signals regarding what they want.

Be it as a tiny seed or as a tall tree, plants take the help of their friends at every step of their lives. Sometimes they use the services of such friends to settle in areas they would otherwise never have been able to visit. At other times they use the services of friends to drive away their enemies. In fact, plants sometimes maintain an army to patrol their borders! They arrange for the army's boarding as well as food.

Let's take a close look at the friends that plants have and how these friends help the plants to survive and spread.

CHAPTER ONE

# Come to Me!

Because we can speak, we can invite our friends home. All we need to do is say, "Come over." But how do plants send out this message to their friends? How do plants say, "Come to me?" It may not be easily evident but it is certain that they do.

Isn't the plant saying, "Come to me?"

Many insects regularly visit flowers. It is a common enough sight to see a beautiful butterfly hovering over a colourful flower. Even the not-so-beautiful moths that fly in the dark, visit the flowers that bloom at night. But how do the moths and butterflies zero in on the flowers? How is it that they unerringly make their way, even to the most inconspicuous blossom while ignoring huge man-made structures alongside? We never see butterflies (except one that may have lost its way) in a shopping mall crowded with humans.

But even an insignificant flowering weed by the roadside does not escape their attention. It is obvious that flowers attract butterflies, birds and bees.

How does the butterfly know where to go?

Where then is the invitation card and how did the message reach the invitees? More importantly, why do flowers call out at all? Do they call out to any and every bird or beast crawling by? After all, we would not let each and every stranger enter our house and serve him or her refreshments, would we? No, and neither do the plants. Plants are selective about the friends they entertain, and though insects make up the majority of their friends, some plants count birds bees and bats as their friends as well. There is a reason why plants are so fond of these visitors.

## Why do plants need friends?

We all know that living beings leave behind their young ones so that their species continue even as individuals die. Plants are living beings too and they are governed by the same rules. Most plants produce seeds that germinate to give rise to tiny plants.

Pollination is the step that leads to the formation of the seeds. Pollination is the transfer of the pollen from one flower to the female reproductive organ of another flower of the same kind. This leads to fertilisation and, ultimately, the formation of seeds. It is also the reason why plants reach out to make friends.

Since most plants are rooted and cannot move about, they recruit agents to do the moving for them. Busy insects, flying birds and hungry bats are all great travellers. So they are just perfect for the job. They scurry about. In the process, they courier the plant's pollen. In return, plants feed them a little nectar and sometimes a bit of the pollen too. And once the seeds are formed, plants use friends to spread them across new territory.

Greedy eaters and great travellers serve to spread the seeds.

## Doesn't this sound like a bribe?

Not really! Think of it as an incentive or a reward. Sometimes friends may be reluctant to come over to our house. So we tempt them by saying we have a new computer game or that there is a special treat in store for them if they come. Well, plants, like us, are not above rewarding their friends to pay a visit. It could

Nectar is yummy.

even be seen as a fee that is paid for a service that the plant receives. We could also call it a bonus or a prize.

## What sort of rewards do plants offer?

The rewards plants pay may take the form of nectar — an energy-rich drink. Sometimes they even provide pollen as a treat.

## How does it work?

Plants produce nectar in nectaries. Nectar is mostly sugar water. It also contains some vitamins, minerals and amino acids or the building blocks of proteins. Most insects love it, as do certain larger animals such as shrews, mice and birds. The humming bird and the sunbirds just love the nectar. They can never have enough of it.

In seeking out this nectar, pollinators incidentally transfer pollen from one plant to another. So most plants try to keep their friends happy by providing rewards. Soon the friends learn to put two and two together. They learn to associate the plant with free food. The bond of friendship is sealed. In exchange, they (unknowingly) carry out a job or two for the plants. After all, it is the spirit of generous give-and-take that characterises friendship, isn't it?

## Is nectar the only reward plants hand out to their friends?

No. Incentives also take the shape of pollen grains. Pollen grains are precious from the plant's point of view. These are not meant to be wasted. However, most plants make copious amounts of it. Some of it goes to feed their friends who love this nutrient-rich powder. Since bees, bats and other friends search for more pollen, they collect quite a bit of it on their bodies. As they fly from flower to flower, they help spread the pollen from blossom to blossom and from plant to plant.

This cousin of the jackfruit tree has a good fungal friend.

Bees and birds have always been treated as friends on whom the plants depend. However, recent findings indicate that plants may actually have many more friends about whom we know little. For example, a strange association between a fungus and the *chempedak* tree has recently been reported from Malaysia.

The *chempedak* tree is a close relative of the jackfruit. It produces edible fruit. The *Choanephora* fungus attacks the male flowers dangling from the *chempedak* tree. Because fungi do not produce their own food, they derive their nourishment from the host on which they grow. The *Choanephora* fungus too derives its nourishment from the *chempedak* tree. But it also provides a food reward for the pollinating insects that visit the infected flowers. These are mainly the gall midges which feed on the flowers, both as larvae and as adults. Interestingly the *chempedak* blossoms do not offer the visting insects any nectar. It is almost as if they have outsourced the refreshment requirements of the visitors to the fungus that is parasitic on it.

Fungi have been known to play a role in pollination of the *arrow arum* too. It is parasitic on the *arrow arum* but it provides pollination service by releasing a scent called 'dumpsterone'. Dumpsterone attracts flies, which help in pollination. However, the *arrrow arum* plants do provide refreshments to the visitors, which may sometimes snack on the fungus as well.

## But what happens when plants stop flowering?

Different flowering species of plants take turns to flower. This ensures that throughout the year, their special friends have something to feed upon. Thus, their friends never starve, although in some seasons food may be less easily available than in other seasons. But then, the lives of butterflies and moths are short and generally coincide with the season of profuse flowering. So, in that brief span of time, they do enjoy the season of plenty.

Some birds and bats seem to instinctively realise that certain flowers are good only at certain times of the year, not throughout. They simply follow the flowering plants, wherever such plants are found. They shift their loyalties from one that has stopped flowering to one that has begun to flower. In doing so, they may cover huge distances and follow a specific route every year. They have established what scientists call, 'nectar corridors'. This means they have worked out a migratory route to take advantage of the different plants coming into bloom at different times. This sequence of flowering plants provides them with an energy-rich drink to fuel their long-distance flights. In essence, they are simply, 'following the food', so to say.

Bats are sensible, not batty at all. They follow nectar corridors all over the globe and so, never go hungry.

One major nectar corridor extends from southwest Mexico to the USA and Canada. The lesser long-nosed bats, rufus hummingbirds, white-winged doves and monarch butterflies as well as many other pollinators follow this route. They move seasonally along this corridor while travelling to their northern breeding grounds and back.

Nectar-feeding lesser long-nosed bats depend upon *agave* and *cactus* nectar for much of the year. They switch to the nectar of other trees and shrubs in winter. These bats are known as 'mobile links', because they provide pollination services between plant populations over long distances.

Cacti that grow in deserts can provide food and shelter to birds and small animals.

White-winged doves pass the summer in the Sonoran Desert, and the winter in Mexico. These are important pollinators of the *saguaro* plants. Over many generations, the doves have synchronised their trip to the desert with the flowering of cacti. Their reproduction is matched with the ripening of the *saguaro* fruit so that their young have sufficient food. Even if one plant stops flowering for a while, other plants provide food to the many friends of plants. It is clear to anyone who observes that all life on Earth is inter-dependent. Even if the links are not clearly visible, we are all linked together in a giant web of life. Disturbing any one link has a serious effect on all others.

## How can the plants ensure that 'rewards' pay off?

An incentive is paid to ensure that a certain service is facilitated. But once in a while, it happens that though the reward is collected, the service is not provided. Now, the question is, what happens if pollen from one plant falls on a flower belonging to another species? Or what happens if say, *sunflower* pollen falls on the *dahlia* flower, thanks to a hungry insect that has visited both the flowers? The *sunflower* pollen would be wasted. Plants have many strategies to ensure that such wastage does not occur.

For one, they have 'friends' who never go to any other plant. These are exclusive friends — a little like the best friend we have in school. Plants have managed to make such 'best friends' by simply making sure that the pollen or nectar is stored at a depth that only the beak-length or tongue-length of its best friend can reach. Of course, this matching of beak-length to the depth of the nectaries took thousands of years to achieve. But once that was achieved, it simply meant that the pollinating friend was best matched with the flower. So the pollinator stays faithful to the flower and both remain happy, each helping the other out.

Reaching the nectar is like winning a hurdle race.

Generosity is a way of ensuring loyalty too. If our friends eat heartily each time they visit our house, it is practically certain they will not immediately stop to eat again elsewhere. If the pollen and nectar rewards are sufficiently large, the friends remain loyal to the flower and do not visit other species. This is, of course, exactly what the plant wants. It guarantees that its pollen will find its way to a flower of the same species.

The *traveller's palm* has only one 'best friend'.

Sometimes friends have specialised powers that prevent other species from moving in. The ruffled lemur found in Madagascar is a very special friend of the *traveller's palm*. This is an ornamental tree that looks like a banana tree except that its leaves are spread out like a fan. Its flowers have strong protective sheaths, which no other animal, except the ruffled lemur, can pull apart to reach the pollen. Over the ages, these two species have forged a strong bond of inter-dependence.

But not all plants like the idea of having just a single exclusive friend. They seem to go out of the way to ensure that they attract more than just one type of friend. Flowers are sometimes arranged in complex formations that virtually guarantee that a bee cannot easily harvest all its blossoms. This makes sense because having just one bee pollinate the flowers would severely restrict the range. How much territory can one single bee cover anyway? A group of bees would certainly cover a much larger area. It is definitely more fun if many friends come to our party. So, why restrict the number of friends to just one? Plant behaviour endorses a similar way of thinking.

## How do plants call out to their friends?

To understand how the message is sent, we have to take a close look at the flower that sends out the invitation. Flowers are of different types. Flowers such as the *dahlia* or *sunflower* are colourful yet without scent. Flowers such as the *jasmine* are strongly scented. The *sweet pea* is both beautifully coloured as well as sweetly scented. Does this have anything to do with the invitation sent out and the visitors they receive? Yes!

Bright colours and strong scent are floral advertisements at work.

The colours and the scent serve as a beacon or a signpost to the visitors. Colours are the way flowers attract the bees and the butterflies. Just as we draw a map to guide our friends to our house, flowers too advertise their presence by means of colour and scent. And just as we serve refreshments to our visitors when they arrive, flowers offer nectar (to drink) and pollen (to eat to) to their visitors.

## How exactly does the scented invitation work?

When we think about the *Rajnigandha* (*rajni* means 'night' and *gandha* means 'scented') or *tube rose* and *raat ki rani* (queen of the night) or the *jasmine*, we realise just how strong the scent can be. It is the way plants draw attention to themselves.

Bee motto: Follow your nost to reach the flower.

Plants cannot speak but their strongly-scented flowers ensure that their message is spread far and wide. There is plenty of variation in the enticing scents that the flowers produce. Beetles like the scents to be fruity or spicy. Bees like the typically sweet scents we call 'floral' or 'flowery'. Bats appreciate flowers with musty aromas.

Flowers produce the type of scents their friends like best.

Flowers seem to know when their friends are likely to be around. Different flowers emit their scents at different times. *Foxglove* flowers that use bees for pollination release four times more scent during the day than they do at night. On the other hand, *Nicotiana*, that depends more on the night-flying moths, is most fragrant after dusk.

Plants are quite sensible about using their scents. They seem to know all about timing. Newly opened buds do not smell as strongly as the mature flowers that are ready to be pollinated. Once pollination is over and the flower has been fertilised, it gives out less fragrance. The little scent it does make is of low grade. Does this not remind you of the food you get if you go to your friend's house the day after the party is over?

Plants certainly don't want to feed friends once their usefulness is over. It sounds very calculating and selfish but the plants now need all their resources to make the fruits, so they wouldn't want to squander anything they might need later.

## Why do some flowers smell rotten?

Interestingly enough, the scents that flowers release need not always be sweet to smell. Many bugs eat rotten flesh or crawl happily on faecal matter. So there are many plants that produce odours that mimic the stink. The giant *Amorphophallus* flower produces a scent like that of rotting fish. The *western skunk cabbage* gets its name from the stinking scent it produces. The beautiful yellow flowers of the common *Mexican poppy* that grows by the Indian roadside produces an awful stench too. The purple *Trillium* flowers have a scent exactly like that of rotting meat. So repulsive is the stench of its cousin, the *red Trillium*, that botanists have nicknamed these, 'Stinking Benjamins'.

*Amorphophallus* flower produces a scent like that of rotting fish.

But perhaps, the crown for producing a stink should go to *Helicodiceros*, which not only grows in areas

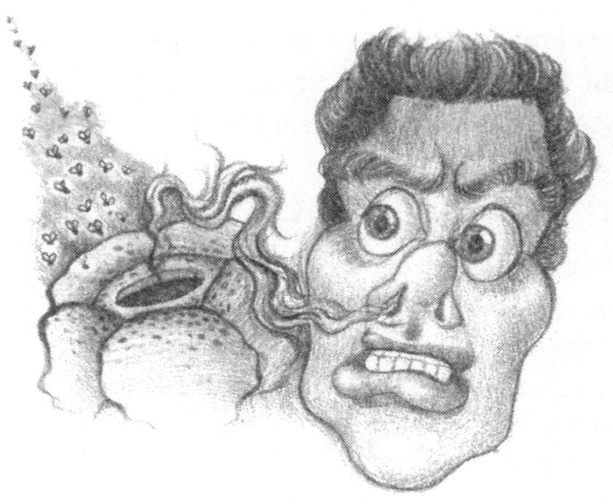

Terrible stench say humans; lovely fragrance say blowflies.

where gulls nest, but which smells like one too. Gulls' nests are messy and are littered with smelly things. Half-eaten rotting fish, decaying fish bones, dead chicks, bad eggs and regurgitated food are all present in the nest of an average gull. As you can imagine, the smell is appalling, to put it mildly. But the blowflies and beetles love the stink the *Helicodiceros* produces. Perhaps the smell reminds them of rotting flesh on which they feast and so they flock to these flowers.

The *voodoo lily* is doubly repulsive to human senses. Not only does it have a stalk of flowers wrapped in a purplish-black leaf that looks like rotting flesh or dung but its smell matches its looks too. It, however, drives flies into a frenzy of excitement wherever it blooms. The flies flock to it even though humans are repulsed by the smell and looks of the plant.

It matters not that humans find some of the scents unbearable — you see, the scent is *not meant* for us! It is meant for the friends of plants and those friends simply love the odour. Just as we remember which of our friends like sweet *lassi* and which of them like theirs with rocksalt, flowers too know what their friends like and provide them with irresistible scents custom-made to their liking.

## Can you guess who comes knocking at this flower's door?

Once we begin to see the plant's point of view and learn a little about the habits of their friends, we could certainly make a very good guess too!

Beetles like white, reddish-brown or dull flowers. They are not graceful in flight and do not manoeuvre well while flying. So they appreciate large, flat, and bowl-shaped flowers. These flowers usually have a foul odour and a little nectar. Flies like dull red or brown flowers with foul odours, especially those that smell like rotten meat. Butterfly-loving flowers open during the day because that is when butterflies are up and about. They are colourful and rich in nectar. Children sometimes pick out the individual flowers from a head of *Ixora* and suck the nectar from it — so copious is the amount. Moth-loving flowers bloom at night and are usually whitish in colour so as to stand out in the dark and possess a strong sweet smell. These may be small in size and clustered together in a bunch.

Trees that rely on bat pollination have night-blooming, whitish, fragrant flowers that produce a lot of high-energy nectar. The flowers are often shaped like pompoms to powder the bat with a dusting of pollen!

They also produce oodles of pollen because they need to have some left over for fertilisation after the hungry bats have had their fill. Bat-pollinated flowers are strongly attached to the stems, usually in a spot free of branches, like a trunk of a tree or a big branch. The flowers are sturdy and firmly attached to withstand the force of the bat's landing and feeding. Their structure and position allow easy landing and take off. Fruit bats are notoriously poor at landing and would destroy the flowers not specially adapted to them!

Flowers that attract birds are usually coloured red, yellow or orange. These have a copious store of nectar. Flowers that call out to insects are usually blue. These have lesser amounts of nectar since the insect appetite is small as compared to that of birds.

Of course, these are all 'rules of the thumb' and close observation is needed to actually list all the friends a flower may have. Nature is subtle in her ways and plants are low-key by nature. Why don't you make a list of the flowering plants in your neighbourhood and try to guess who their friends are?

## How do insects find their way to the fragrant flowers?

All insects that respond to the invitation sent out in the form of scent follow it to the source. The trick to fly correctly is simple. The nearer they come to the flower, the stronger is the scent and the further they go, the weaker does the scent become. So how do they find their way to the flowers? They just follow their noses! And sometimes, following their noses can lead to strange situations too. What usually happens is that when the host is overenthusiastic, the rules of hospitality mean prison for the guests.

## Do some flowers lock up their visitors?

Some plants do!

Plants like the *arum lilies* have tiny flowers, clustered together along a fleshy pole and partially surrounded by a leaf. They send out the smell of rotten fish or faeces. Swarms of flies arrive, expecting a feast. It is then that the plant plays a nasty trick. It traps the flies inside a chamber at the base of the leaf that protects the fertile flowers. The flies try to escape and in the process, their bodies get a dusting of pollen. The fleshy pole finally wilts and the flies find a way out but not before pollinating the flowers, which is why the plant had invited the flies in the first place.

*Arum lilies* send out the smell of rotten fish or faeces.

It just shows, doesn't it, that we must exercise care when answering invitations! However, none of the flies are hurt. On the contrary, they spend the night warmly cocooned from the chill of the night. Skunk cabbages also pull off a similar trick.

The *cuckoopint plant* has a comparable way of ensuring successful pollination. It traps its insect friends by means of downward-pointing hairs inside its swollen base. As the insect slides down, it collects the pollen on its body. The downward pointing hairs foil its attempts to climb up and out. The frustrated insect walks around inside, brushing past female flowers. As it does so, pollen from the insect's body brushes on to the female flowers and fertilises them. Later, at night, the plant allows the insect to escape.

## Do some plants drug their friends too?

Well, some plants do have a notorious reputation and some do appear to drug their friends. But the one argument to be made in favour of such behaviour is that they do not hurt or kill their visitors. That would rather, in any case, defeat the purpose from the plant's point of view.

The yellow petal on the *lady-slipper orchids* bears a kind of pouch, inside which is found a chemical that flies find irresistible. They buzz over it and land near the opening of the pouch. Then they begin crawling all over the flower. During their explorations, they often climb over the edge and fall inside the pouch. The chemical inside the pouch has a powerful effect on them. It makes them act as if they are drunk! The 'drugged' flies fly blindly around in the prison till they notice two 'escape windows' in the pouch. On the way out, the plant sticks pollen sacs to their backs.

Interestingly, the flies appear to be none the worse for the experience they have had. Maybe, they even 'enjoy' the experience for they simply head for the next orchid. The process of drugged imprisonment is repeated and the pollen sacs from the first visit are removed by the stigma of the second orchid. Pollination is achieved!

## Do plants pretend to be female insects by smelling and looking like one?

As crazy as it sounds, it is nevertheless true! Strictly speaking, this is actually a form of cheating. It appears, doesn't it, that plants, like humans, cheat too?

*Orchids* are the most celebrated frauds in the plant kingdom. Some *orchid* flowers have managed, over the millennia, to evolve in such a way that they look like female insects. This is called 'mimicking'. Many male insects are fooled into thinking they have found a wife. They flock to such flowers. They pick up huge amounts of pollen as they buzz around the so-called female. They then transport this pollen to the next mimic they find. Some of the mimics are really good — they even smell like a real female of the species. No wonder the male insects are fooled!

Is this an orchid or is it Mrs Bee?

However, we must admit that plants do not deliberately cheat. It is not that the thought comes to them or that they decide to manipulate others for their own gain. It is likely that the trait emerged by chance, thousands of years ago and plants benefited from it. So this trait persisted. Over the ages, evolution polished it. Today this mimicry is probably the key to its survival. But what would happen, if the insect it mimics, dies out? As it so often happens to those who hitch their wagon to a solitary star, it would probably lead to the plant's doom as well. Having just one friend is not a good strategy, no matter how good the friendship is.

## How are coloured invitations different from scented ones?

Colours are important invitations too, but these are targeted at a different group of friends. Birds are attracted by colour but very few species of birds can appreciate scents. Plants that prefer birds as their special friends, therefore do not bother much with producing scents, either sweet or foul. Instead they have evolved warm hues. They come in beautiful reds, oranges and yellows. This emphasis on the red and yellow colours is because the eyes of birds are most sensitive to red.

The difference in colours is often a clear indication as to the kind of friends the flower has. Even related flowers, such as the red *Delphiniums* and the blue *Delphiniums* attract different friends, thanks to their differences in colours. Hummingbirds visit the red *Delphinium* but only the bees, that cannot see the colour red at all, check out the blue *Delphiniums.*

Those flowers that bloom by night are usually white

in colour so that they stand out in the dark and can be easily spotted. White or pale colours are easy to spot at night and bats and moths have no trouble in finding their way to such flowers.

## Why don't birds and insects visit the same flowers?

Insects too can see colour, though they do not perceive them exactly the way we do.

The beaks of humming birds are perfect for the flowers they like to visit.

Light covers a range called the 'spectrum'. We see things in what is called the visible part of the spectrum. It does not include the ultraviolet and infrared parts of the spectrum. The part of the spectrum in which insects can see is slightly different from ours. It lies in the ultraviolet range.

To know how a flower actually appears to an insect, scientists photograph flowers using a camera that works in the ultraviolet range. It is that part of the spectrum that the insect's eyes are sensitive to. The results are incredible! In photographs we can often see coloured dots and dashes on the petals. These are called 'honey guides'. Such markings are invisible to the human eye. The markings appear very similar to the markings on the airport runways. It is almost as if the petals are the runways on which the insect aircraft is expected to land and that the plant has made arrangements for its safe landing.

Scientists are still debating if the flowers evolved to match the sensitivity of insect eyes or if insect eyes evolved to see all the colours of the flowers. What we do know is that like good friends, flowers and insects meet each other halfway. So now we know that flower colour is not meant to please human eyes but the eyes of insects and birds!

## Are colours and scents the only way a flower calls out to friends?

Colour and scent are the two primary means by which flowers attract attention, but these are not the only two ways. The basic idea is to catch the attention of friends.

Tiny flowers manage to do this by clustering together to present a more 'showy' look. At other times, colourful petal-like structures, called 'bracts', surround insignificant flowers. A common example is the *Bougainvillea*. The actual flower of the *Bougainvillea* is tiny. What we commonly and mistakenly take to be the colourful flowers are actually the three papery bracts surrounding the flower and drawing attention to it. It is a little like an ordinary-looking person appearing gorgeous, thanks to a little cosmetic effort or standing out in a crowd by wearing an outlandish hat! But that is the crux of the matter anyway, because if our friends do not know if we exist or where we are, how will they visit us?

Then again, some plants are really smart. They use technology! But, of course, their technology has been shaped, not by directed research or effort, but by evolution over thousands of years.

The *Macuna holtoni* is a cousin to the peas we eat. This is a climbing vine that grows in Costa Rica. It relies on bats to pollinate it. Bats send out high-pitched sounds that bounce off their targets, providing them with an idea about where the target is. The flowers of *Macuna holtoni* are so shaped that they reflect bat signals from all directions within a 40-degree cone. Now, isn't that a wonderful way of recognising the

The shape of the *Macuna holtoni* flowers help bats find them.

special ability of friends and actually meeting them halfway? Whoever could have thought that speechless flowers could communicate with bats that speak a 'language' most humans cannot hear? Just goes to show that the best communicators need not make a big noise about it!

## How does the flower make the friend comfortable?

Once the attention of the friend is caught and a visit assured, the first step the flower takes is to provide a stable 'landing platform' for its winged friends. While colour patterns and honeyguides help the oncoming aerial visitor to the correct 'flight path', a landing platform ensures a safe landing.

Landing platforms are particularly important for those birds and insects that cannot hover in mid-flight like a helicopter. These, like Jumbo jets, definitely need a place to alight. Beetles, in particular, are clumsy fliers and beetle-pollinated flowers need easy entrances if a crash landing is to be avoided. Wouldn't you need a wide entrance if you kept an elephant for a pet? So do flowers have all sorts of shapes to facilitate the visits of their friends. Sometimes they are shaped in such a way that no others except the 'best friends' can find their way to their stores of nectar and pollen. It is like having the specific key to a treasure trove. Those that do not hold the key can never hope to open the chest and find the goodies.

The *kangaroo paw* flowers provide a perch for their feathered friends.

But plants are generous towards friends. The *kangaroo paw* is a plant that grows, you guessed it, in Australia. It bears lily-like flowers. Birds can usually stand on the ground and extend their necks to poke their beaks right into the flowers. But some *kangaroo-paws* grow quite tall. The birds cannot then sip nectar while standing on the ground. To accommodate these birds, the flower-bearing stems are strong enough to bear the weight of the birds along with the weight of the flowers.

Flowers that attract hovering birds, such as the hummingbird, usually have bell-shaped flowers that point downward. But sometimes the colourful flowers point up. This is an invitation to perching birds. And indeed, the reddish leaves around the purple flowers of *Tillandsia* are very stiff and provide the needed resting pad for perching birds. It is almost as if the plants are providing a safe perch to the birds. We do similar things, don't we? Don't we provide cushions to raise the height of a chair in case a child has to share the table with us during a meal?

The landing platform of milkweed flowers force butterflies into an awkward position and dust them with pollen.

But plants are sometimes smart enough to use discomfort as a strategy to gain what they want. Butterflies are the chosen friends of the *milkweed*. Most flowers that rely on butterflies usually have a landing pad or perch. But *milkweed* flowers have a very small landing platform. This forces the butterfly to land with its legs between the cup-shaped petals, each of which holds a droplet of nectar. Now, just where the legs grasp the flower stalk lies the pollen-containing anther, coated with a sort of 'super-glue'.

As the butterfly flies off, it carries a cargo of pollen sacs glued to its legs. When the butterfly lands on the next flower, the pollen sacs come off and pollination is achieved.

Just as a warm room is wonderful to step into if the night is cold, plants too seem to recognise this fact. Some plants, notably the *arum lilies* and the *sacred lotus* can actually raise their temperatures. They can keep the high temperature at a steady 30°-35° Celsius. Initially scientists were puzzled by this fact. Then they rationalised that heating the flowers meant that the scented oils would vaporise better and so enhance the dispersal of scents. But as they studied the phenomenon more closely, they realised that the elevated temperature was the plant's way of helping out its friends — the beetles.

Insects aid pollination as they beetle along.

Beetles need to warm up to about 30° Celsius before they can fly. To reach this temperature, beetles are forced to shiver violently so that their muscles are warmed up. This shivering consumes a lot of energy. What plants such as the *sacred lotus* offer is the chance to land on a warm flower and draw the heat from it. In the human context too, it is not difficult to decide on a winter night whether we wish to enter a cold and chilly room where the only way to keep warm would be to rub our palms together, or a room that has a lovely glowing fireplace. The lowly beetle knows and recognises a good deal when it finds one, so that the friendship between beetles and warmth-providing plants is sealed easily.

CHAPTER TWO

# Conquering New Lands

Once pollination is achieved, the plant focuses its attention on producing seeds. Seeds are marvellous things as they signify both the beginning and the end. They represent a new beginning because locked away inside a seed lies a brand new plant. The huge *oak* tree that you now see was a tiny acorn once. The *mango* tree that spreads its branches far and wide was once contained in the stone (seed) you held in your hands as you sucked the juicy yellow pulp. Given the requisite care they need, seeds sprout and ultimately grow into new plants. Some plants die after they produce the seeds and even if they don't, seeds also represent the end of a cycle.

Seeds need to be spread far and wide. In fact, most grow best away from the parent plant. This is because an established tree almost always commands the best for itself. It is taller than the sapling and so catches most of the sun, while the baby plant struggles in the shadow of the mother tree. It has deeper roots and so corners most of the available water. Hence, it is definitely better for a seed to travel on — away from its birthplace to set down roots elsewhere.

## Seeds do not have limbs.

Nature has provided wind and water which act as agents of transport to carry the seeds to faraway places. But wind and water are capricious. One cannot order them about nor predict their behaviour. It is definitely better to have friends whose behaviour pattern ensures that they will carry the seeds to greener pastures. Once again, plants forge links with the birds and the beasts to carry their seeds to places where these can take root and grow.

## How do seeds hitch a ride?

Some seeds are absolutely direct in their approach. They bear hooks and burrs on their surface and when the animals graze, the hooks and burrs get attached to the animal's fur. This strategy is particularly successful if the animal has a thick coat. Sheep can pick up hundreds of these hooked seeds. Thus the seeds go everywhere the animal does. They usually fall off when the animal brushes against something. Sometimes the seeds cause itching and the animal actually rubs its body till the offending seeds fall off. The fruits of the *cocklebur*, *spear grass* and *love grass* are common examples. They even stick to clothes if you walk through a field where these grow and may even scratch the uncovered legs. But, perhaps the worst (or best, depending on whether it is the plant's point of view or yours) is the hooked seed capsule of the *African grapple* plant. The capsules have hooked arms that can penetrate even the thick hide of a rhino.

Once the hooks get a firm grip, the capsule stays on till movement makes it break and release the seeds. So strong is the grip that this plant is also called the *devil's claw.* Obviously the experience is not a pleasant one, even for the proverbially thick-skinned rhino, though the trick works for the plant. However, most plants are subtler in their approach. After all, you can catch more flies with a spoonful of honey than with a cupful of vinegar.

Ouch! That hurts!!

## So, do plants offer more rewards?

Yes, they do. And it is a reward you and I have willingly accepted, though we have not always kept our end of the bargain.

*Litchies* and *oranges*, *grapes* and *pears*, *papayas* and *melons*, *cherries* and *mangoes* — name a fruit you like and scientists will tell you it is an incentive. Most plants enclose their seeds inside a fleshy and tasty envelope. This is the fruit we eat. Fruits enclose seeds. A plant cannot speak but its intentions speak louder than words ever could. The very idea behind having fruits is to attract friends. Inherent is the hope that they will either spit out or pass out the seeds somewhere, away from the mother plant. It is a gamble actually: a hope that chance will favour it and it will find fertile land, adequate water and sunshine wherever it falls. Till not so long back, this was a risk worth taking. After all, this is how all the natural forests of the world had once sprung up. But this is a losing battle in today's concrete jungles, which we call 'cities', where a patch of bare soil is rarely seen. But if conditions are what Nature has intended them to be, then the behaviour reaps rich rewards.

## How do fruits help attract friends?

Fruits are sour or tart when immature but sweet and juicy when ripe. Unripe fruits are usually green and remain hidden among the green leaves. But when the fruit becomes ripe, it changes colour to red or yellow. Both are colours that stand out vividly against the green leaves. Birds and other animals can spot these easily. Also a ripe fruit smells wonderful though unripe fruits may have no smell to speak of. Haven't you seen adults pick up a melon or a mango and sniff it before buying? What they are trying to do is to find out which melon or mango, amongst the many that the fruit-seller has on his cart, is the one that will be the sweetest and the tastiest. Of course, in today's world of cold storage and artificial ripening, relying on your nose alone may not quite yield the result you are looking for. But habits die hard and even in departmental stores you would come across matrons with their noses pressed to even cellophane-covered fruits on display. However, under natural conditions and in the wild, most animals make the best use of this faculty.

Most humans tend to think that the 'best' alone is fit for human consumption. And whatever is 'not fit' for human consumption would serve the animals well enough. However, this is faulty reasoning. Under natural conditions, animals spend hours foraging for the best. When food is in plenty, animals can be really choosy about what they eat. They spend a long time selecting a fruit and will throw away those that do not meet their high standards. Sometimes the fruit may be discarded after a single tentative bite. And if they throw it strongly enough, the fruit (with seeds inside) might land in new territory. And as ripe fruits are usually tender, such fruits will burst, splattering the seeds, which may germinate and grow if conditions are right. So, either way, the plant gets what it needs — new territory to conquer.

## How will the seed germinate if the animal has eaten it?

Most seeds pass intact through the guts of the animals. In fact, the pat of faeces serves as a spot of fertiliser for the sprouting seeds. One good deed deserves another, wouldn't you say? This is the way many birds, bats, squirrels, foxes, monkeys and even some insects help disperse the seeds.

Bats are excellent agents when it comes to spreading seeds. Bats ingest the fruit, digest the pulp

surrounding the seeds, and then defecate the seeds. Sometimes the process takes less than 20 minutes. Bats often defecate the seeds while in flight. Many plants that use bats as agents of dispersal are often the first plants to move into large open areas. They are the first colonisers of new space.

Bats defecate seeds while flying from one place to another.

This phenomenon is not easy to observe as bats are nocturnal animals.

They are active when we are asleep. So how can we be certain that bats contribute to seed dispersal? Scientists have carried out a simple experiment to study it. They placed plastic sheets in the middle of clear fields. They found that there was a sharp difference during the day and night collection rates of seeds. Scarcely any seeds arrived during the day. But during the night there was a steady 'seed rain', thanks to bat activity.

Bats spread seeds more widely because they defecate as they fly. Birds usually defecate while they roost or perch. This means that bats tend to disperse seeds over cleared land, while birds do it where there are trees. In this way, bats help the forest expand and tree seedlings to take over cleared land.

Bats also spread more seeds because they eat more fruit. A bat can often eat more than its own weight!

Most carry the fruits in their mouths as they fly. Some bats have cheek pouches to stuff the fruit into. The cheek pouches of Whalberg's epauletted fruit bat are simply enormous. Large amounts of fruits can be stuffed into them to be consumed in flight. By knocking down fruits as they eat, fruit bats also supply fruit pieces to ground-dwelling fruit-eaters, which in turn help spread the seeds in areas they roam.

We usually tend to think of climbing or flying animals as those that would reach the fruits and spread the seeds. Monkeys and birds come readily to mind in this context. However, ground-dwelling animals also help in spreading the seeds. Ripe fruits naturally detach from the tree and splatter as they hit the ground. The impact spreads the seeds a little. It also allows ground-dwelling animals to eat the ripe mess on the ground. Sometimes an animal takes advantage of another animal's behaviour by snatching the fruit and this works to the advantage of the plant.

Langurs are fussy and wasteful eaters. They dislodge or throw away more fruit than they eat. Chital deer have worked this out to their advantage. They just follow the langurs. And when the langurs feast on the treetops, the chitals feast on the ground too. The tree is happy too. There are two species of animals that act as agents in the dispersal of seeds.

Animals we would never associate with a tree are often its dispersal agents. The barking deer or Indian muntjac, for example, disperses the seeds of the *hog plum.* The fruit has a high protein and calcium content and the barking deer swallows it whole. Amazingly,

Langurs do not believe in the saying, 'Waste not, want not.'

the seeds are vomited out undamaged after several hours of rumination and germinate well, clearly none the worse for wear after travelling through the barking deer's stomach! Barking deer are important dispersal agents for other large-seeded woody plants, including the *amla*.

The rhino is a dispersal agent for the *trewia* tree as well as for certain kinds of grasses. The seeds of the *trewia* tree are hard and large and rhinos apparently enjoy eating these. However, there are always one or two seeds that escape being chewed up in the rhino's mouth and which pass unscathed through its guts. The pat of rhino dung ensures nourishment for the seed as it grows into a sapling.

Rhinos are creatures of habit and they defecate only in certain areas. The riverbank that the rhino uses as a toilet therefore becomes the range of the *trewia* tree. The same story is repeated for the grasses the rhino eats. This story has two happy endings, one for the grass and the *trewia* and the other for the rhino. For the grass and *trewia* it means continuation of the species; it means survival. For the rhino it means more food; it also means survival.

In the final analysis this is what all friendship is all about — survival!

## Does the plant do anything to 'speed up' things?

Well, yes, it does. Some seeds have a covering that acts as a laxative. Eating too many ripe *guavas* at one sitting could have an embarrassing outcome even for humans. *Guava* seeds are one of the many types of seeds that pass undamaged even through the human gut! Other seeds are bowel irritants. Either way, the plant sees to it that seeds do not remain inside the animal's guts for too long. Seeds that pass through the guts of animal friends are usually designed to be tough. These generally have a thick coat that provides protection to the 'embryo' inside from the chewing action of teeth and the acidic stomach fluids.

## What qualities does the plant look for in a friend?

It helps if the friends occupy a wide area or home range. The larger the territory the animal regards as its own, the larger does the extended home range of the plant become. The animal helps to spread the seeds over its entire range. This is a blessing indeed for a rooted plant that is unable to move about.

Sometimes the habits of certain animals work in favour of the plants. Squirrels, for example, are well known for collecting nuts, cones and acorns and hiding these to store them. They often bury many small caches in preparation for winter when food becomes scarce. However, these animals never store fruits because fruits would rot. In any case, those plants that produce seeds in the form of nuts and cones have much to be thankful for. The squirrels and their cousins, the chipmunks, are quite forgetful. Often they forget where they have buried their cache. Undisturbed, the seeds in the buried cache sprout in the next season. Soon a lovely new sapling or two are seen swaying in the breeze where none had been present earlier.

I hope I remember where my cache is.

Ants too carry out a similar function. Some ants are great hoarders. They are called 'harvesting ants' as they collect seeds from grasses and cereals and store them in large underground nests. They seem to know that germination of the seed means that the potential for storage of seeds is lost. So they keep biting off the emerging roots. They even periodically sun the seeds to dry them out and delay germination.

It is a running battle between the seed's need to germinate and the ant's need to prevent germination. When the ants realise that a particular seed has germinated despite their attempts to prevent it, they bring it up to the surface and throw it away. Perhaps they do so to keep their hill clean. But this act is a blessing for the plant. It gets the sunlight so essential for its growth. The seed now goes on to grow into an adult plant. Soon there is a 'garden' growing around the anthill. These plants produce seeds, some of which the ants glean. The cycle goes on. Both the ants and the plants thrive.

Other plants also seem to know that ants store provisions for a rainy day. These plants produce seeds covered with an oily covering called 'eliasome'. Ants love eating the eliasome. Whenever they find eliasome-covered seeds, they drag them down into their nests to eat at leisure. The interesting part is that the eliasome diet is so tasty, that the ants do not even nibble on the seeds; they just leave it underground. Again, this is what the seeds want — a bit of moist soil to germinate in. And they do just that!

These are good friendships based on beneficial behaviour patterns which assure solid returns to both the friends.

There are examples of behaviour-based friendship from the fungi kingdom (though, strictly speaking, fungi are not plants) too and these involve ants as well. The leaf-cutter ant gets its name from its behaviour. True to its name, the ant specialises in cutting large sections of leaves and carrying these like green flags to its nest. It is quite a sight to see long columns of ants, each carrying a green banner and marching in a straight line to the nest. You would almost expect to hear a military band playing! Once inside the nest, the green leaves are cut into smaller and smaller pieces. These tiny pieces are used to line the floor of the chambers inside the nest. Soon the white thread-like branches of the fungus begin to grow on the rotting leaves.

The ants tend to the fungus carefully. They act almost as the human gardeners do. The surprising finding about leaf-cutter ants as a group is that though they grow several kinds of fungus, each species of leaf-cutter ant specialises in growing just one kind of fungus. So, inside a particular nest, we find only one kind of fungus, though an adjacent nest may well be home to a different sort of fungus. The fungus too seems to recognise the care the ants provide. In return, it pays the ants for the services offered.

Ants tend their gardens well.

Tiny rounded bodies called 'bromatia' appear on the fungus and the leaf-cutter ants feed solely on these. The better care they take of the fungus, the more are the rewards that follow. So every morning the leaf-cutter ants set out to cut out more leaves to bring back to the nest as food for the fungus, which in return produces food for them.

CHAPTER THREE

# Army and Warfare!

All living beings on Earth have some means of protection because survival is important in Nature. Every living species has predators that prey on it. Many animals graze on plants and some animals may even uproot a plant and eat all of it. Others lay eggs on their leaves. When the young larvae emerge, they immediately begin chomping on the leaves and flowers. This may cause tremendous damage and even kill the plant. From the plant's point of view such situations are best avoided. But then, rooted as most plants are, it is impossible to flee when an enemy approaches.

Want to risk a bite?

So, some keep an army of ants that patrol the tree's branches, viciously stinging all those that approach too near. Other plants release a chemical into the air when attacked. The chemical is usually something that is very attractive to the enemies of the species that have attacked the plant. In employing this strategy, plants are using the adage, 'An enemy's enemy is our friend,' to great advantage.

## Do plants really maintain an army?

Some plants do maintain an army of ants to patrol their branches and lend protection in exchange for food and shelter.

No one messes with an army of ants.

The *Acacia* is the most famous example of plant-ant association. Some species of *Acacia* provide everything that ants may need. This includes specialised structures to house the ants. *Acacia* trees sprout thick, hollow thorns along the branches. These thorns are perfect as barracks for the ant army. Nectar is produced at the base of its leaves. Tiny buttons of protein and oil are produced, especially to feed the ants. All said and done, the ants are housed comfortably and fed extremely well.

The ants that patrol the *Acacia* are highly aggressive. Up to 25 per cent of the ant colony always remains on active duty. The ants serve the plant, day and night; they patrol and clean the plant. They kill insects that land on the *Acacia*. They do not even spare the large herbivores such as giraffes, though, of course, ant bites do not kill them. However, the bites are painful and most such animals avoid the *Acacias* with ants.

All plants sprouting within half a metre of the *Acacia* are at the ant's mercy. The ants chew up such plants, and even any vines that try to grow using the *Acacia* as a support. This aggressive behaviour is a boon for the *Acacia* plants.

*Acacias* need direct sunshine. They also need lots of sunlight to grow well. The action of ants assures a clean area free of encroachments that could force it to share the sunlight. And of course, the taller and bigger an *Acacia* grows, the more food and shelter it provides to the ants. This association is somewhat like working hard for a small company — the bigger it grows, the more assured your employment and perks become!

Scientists once removed the ants on an *Acacia* in an experiment to see what would happen. The plant died within a year. It died because it could not repulse the insect attacks. With ants, an *Acacia* may live for about 20 years. The ants too cannot survive without the *Acacia's* payment of shelter and food. Some *Acacia* species produce toxins to protect themselves instead of having ants. However, these grow slowly as compared to those *Acacias* that are friends to ants.

The *Macaranga* shrub also depends on ants to

protect it. These plants suffer twice the leaf damage and are smothered by almost six to nine times more vines, if the ants are absent. No wonder then that the plant acts as a hospitable host. It provides ants with hollow stems outfitted with entry holes. It also provides a regular supply of special food bodies on the underside of young leaves. The food is rich in glycogen, a carbohydrate normally found only in animals, proteins and lipids. The ants feed these to their larvae. In return, the ants scour the plant for insect eggs. They bite off any climbers that dare touch the plant.

Ants milk aphids or ant-cows for honey dew.

*Tachygalia* is a tree that grows mostly under the shade of bigger trees. It flowers only once before dying. Because the tree grows in shade, sunlight is doubly precious and every leaf counts. This plant also has an alliance with ants. The tree provides hollow leaves as ant shelters. The tree, however, does not provide ants with any food. So the ants 'cultivate' a species of aphids (ant cows) that live off the plant sap. In return, the aphids give out a sweet liquid called 'honeydew' on which the ants love to feed. The *Tachygalia* ants are large and aggressive. To protect their aphid herds, the ants kill other insects that land on the plant and inflict painful bites on large animals.

Some *rattan plants* provide swollen woody chambers for ants. When a *rattan* plant is touched, the ants make a loud rattling sound by beating their jaws against the hollow chamber. The sound is a warning to intruders. The ants also kill any insects that try to eat the *rattan* plant.

The *passion vine* produces nectar at the base of each leaf. The nectar is irresistible to five species of ants. These are active at different times of the day, so the plant gets round-the-clock security. These ants attack other insects and even prune old leaves that no longer produce nectar. The stems of the *vines* become hollow with age and this provides spacious homes to ants and so large colonies thrive here.

In the savannas of Central America, ants hollow out the large thorns of the plant for nests. They feed on sweet secretions from the nectaries at the base of each petiole and on the special protein-rich bodies found on the tips of the leaves. Together these provide an almost complete diet for the ant. In return, they protect the trees. The ants release a nasty odour if the plant is threatened. They also physically attack the herbivore.

*Epiphytes* are plants that grow on other plants but which are not parasitic on them. *Orchids* are good examples of *epiphytes*. These just use the trees as perches but do not depend on them for nutrition. So many *epiphytes* turn to ants, not for protection, but for minerals, which are so scarce in their lofty perch.

Ant-house plants grow as *epiphytes* high up in trees.

Their stems are swollen and riddled with chambers ideal for nesting. The plant even provides ant-sized entrances to these tunnels. The ants not only keep the plant free of insects, but also provide the *epiphyte* with minerals. The plants provide two types of chambers — the first type has smooth walls and the other has rough walls. The ants live in the smooth-walled chambers. They use the rough-walled chambers as a dump for their rubbish. This includes ant faeces and dead ants. Fungus may also grow in these dumps. Fungal activity speeds up decomposition. The nutrients present in ant-rubbish are valuable. The plants have special wart-like growths inside the rough-walled chambers to absorb the nutrients.

The *Tillandsia* plants harbour ants in their central stems. So, instead of directing water droplets towards the central stems, their leaves are designed to channel water away from the centre of the plant. This way the centre of the plant remains dry and habitable for the ants.

There are many other plants that rely on ants. Some *ferns* have swollen, hollow root-like structures that are excellent homes to ants. Other *ferns* even have a series of chambers that act as galleries in which ants live. The *pot-leaf* plant gets its name from the special pot-like leaves it bears alongside the usual leaves. Ants quickly colonise the hollow pot-shaped leaves. Eventually ant-activity fills up the pots with ant debris. The plant then grows roots into the leaf to extract the nutrients.

## Apart from being security gruards, what else do ants do?

Some ants create a garden in a tree or shrub by making a ball of chewed fibres, soil and litter. These 'balls' may range in size from that of a golf ball to a football. The ants then gather and plant seeds in this ball. As the seeds germinate, the ball becomes a sort of ant-garden. Many of the plant species are found only in such gardens and nowhere else.

Plants that are grown by the ants in their gardens often have fleshy seeds. The seeds may also attract ants by smelling like ant larvae or ant prey. These ant gardens are found in the rain-forests of South America as well as in Southeast Asia.

However, a very dramatic example of protection given by ants to their host plants has recently been discovered.

A formidable injection of formic acid kills off plants that the ants do not consider friends.

The *devil's gardens* are large stands of trees (usually the only species that scientists call, *Duroia hirsuta*). It used to be said that an evil forest-spirit cultivated this garden and prevented growth of other trees. It was not till the end of 2005 that scientists discovered that it is a species of ants that poisons all other plants by injecting formic acid — the same chemical that causes itching when ants bite us. The ants use formic acid as a herbicide or a chemical that kills plants.

There is a reason why these ants do this. This particular species lives in the hollow, swollen stems of *Duroia.* By killing other plants, the ants provide future generations with abundant nesting sites. A *devil's garden* begins when the ant queen colonises a single *Duroia* tree. Over the years, the ants clear the area around the main tree and new *Duroia* plantlets take over this area. A *devil's garden* is usually tended by a single colony comprising as many as three million workers and as many as 15,000 queens.

Since ant colonies can live upto 800 years, the strategy to ensure that only the *Duroia* lives and no other begins to make sense from the ant's point of view, doesn't it?

Beetles are not above cheating the plants by pretending to be ants.

## Do plants provide ant-food even if the ants are not around?

Most ant-plants don't produce food packages unless ants actually make their homes in its branches. One such plant is the giant *piper plant.* It is home to tiny ants that live in hollow, curled leaf blades. The ants are too tiny to chase off the insects, so these only clean off the fungus from the leaves and stems. The plant provides food packages rich in protein and fat, but only when ants are actually in residence on its branches and not otherwise.

However, at least one beetle has learnt to mimic the ant's secretions that stimulate the plant to produce the packages, without 'paying' by protecting the plant! There are cheats in the insect kingdom too — to pay back in the same coin the cheats in the plant kingdom!

## How do pollinators bypass ferocious ants?

This is a major problem indeed, but plants have found a way out of this predicament. The need to attract pollinators is an important one. However, it is too much to expect that patrolling ants would discriminate between friendly insects and the unfriendly ones or that they would 'understand' the need for pollination. So how was this paradox resolved? Scientists had long been puzzled by this conflict of interest. Then they stumbled across one clue — they found that ants avoided crawling over young and fresh flowers but not older ones that had already been pollinated. They also realised that on rainy days, the effect seemed to disappear and the ants patrolled new flowers as well.

The scientists wondered if the young flowers exuded some kind of water-soluble ant-repellent that washed away in the rain. To check if this was indeed the case, scientists rubbed a young flower on an old one. True enough, the ants avoided that older flower. Scientists studying this phenomenon felt that some chemical was present in the pollen. Hence, this phenomenon is still being studied.

However, irrespective of where the chemical comes

from, its presence ensures that the fresh flowers are free of ants. Bees and other pollinators seem to know this. They make straight for such flowers with alacrity and thus does the *Acacia* achieve pollination. After pollination, when the repellent wears off, the renewed presence of the ants protects the developing seeds from being eaten.

CHAPTER FOUR

# Strange Friendships and Stranger Warfare

It is said that friends make up for whatever quality is lacking in you. The class-topper may be best friend with someone who is not academically brilliant. Friendship looks for compatibility. Friends complement each other's abilities. Friends rush to the other's rescue when they see that one of them is in trouble or when one's enemy is near. The plant kingdom offers many examples of this.

## Can plants and animals be friends?

Yes, indeed. Sea slugs, which are shell-less marine snails, eat underwater plants such as *algae*. But they do not digest the chloroplasts. By some physiological trick they manage to keep the chloroplasts alive and

Look out for lichens. The presence of lichens on a tree means that the area is reasonably pollution-free.

functional inside their bodies. Since the chloroplasts carry out photosynthesis and produce sugar, the sea slug soon needs to depend less and less on outside food, though, of course, it would still need to snack from time to time to maintain the chloroplast levels in its tissues.

The single-celled slipper animalcule or *Paramecium bursaria* engulfs tiny green algae into vacuoles or empty, sac-like spaces inside its body. It seems to benefit from the food synthesised by the alga because scientists have found that while *Paramecium* can be cultured apart from the alga, it then must be given extra food. The alga appears to benefit from the carbon dioxide produced by *Paramecium* as well as from the *Paramecium*'s ability to travel to spots where there is ample light to carry out photosynthesis.

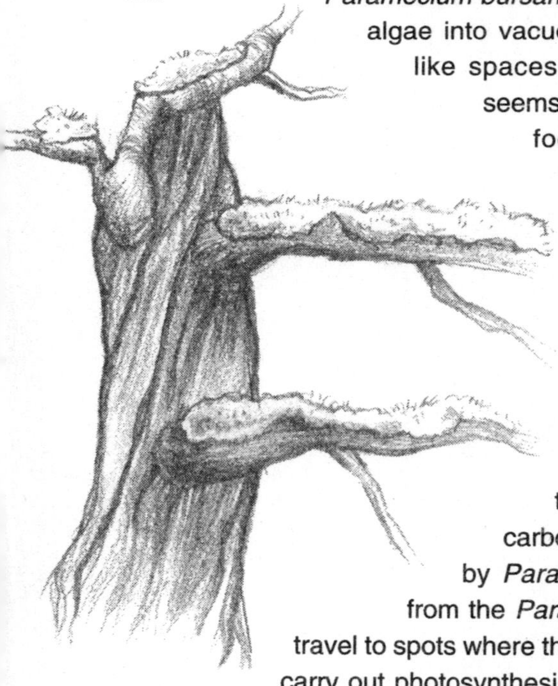

## What are lichens?

Lichens are unusual examples of a plant's ability to make friends. Most of the *lichen* is composed of fungal filaments but living among these filaments are algal cells. The fungus and the alga, which together make the *lichen*, may be capable of living independently. But mostly *lichens* include a fungus that cannot survive on its own, so dependent on its algal partner for survival has it become. In all cases though, the appearance of the fungus in the lichen seems quite different from what it looks like when it grows as an independent species.

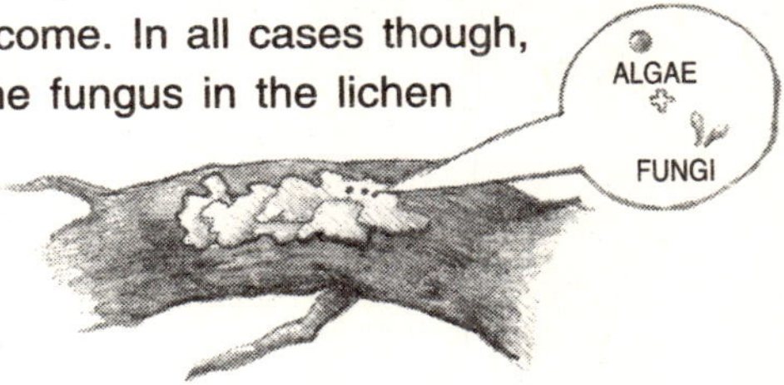

ALGAE

FUNGI

*Lichen* is not a single organism the way most other living things are. Rather, it is a combination of two organisms, which live together so intimately that it becomes difficult to tell where one begins and the other ends. *Lichens* are called 'dual organisms' because they are inter-dependent associations between two entirely different types of life forms. *Lichens* can take on different forms.

*Foliose lichens* have a flat, leaf-like structure, while *Fruticose lichens* have an erect or dangling, bushy structure. *Squamulose lichens* are minute and scalelike and *crustose* lichens produce a flat crust on or beneath the rock or tree surfaces.

Since *lichens* first appeared about 400 million years ago, this is a successful strategy. *Lichens* are the first life forms to appear on barren rocks and this demonstrates just how hardy they are. Interestingly, *lichens* are extremely sensitive to pollution and any area where *lichens* thrive is considered to be pollution-free.

## Can plants call out to friends when in trouble?

"Help me" — this is the universal cry when we are in trouble. And help comes immediately from friends. In fact, all who answer the call are friends. Plants cannot speak a language we can hear, but they do send out distress calls that their friends answer.

Some plants release a signal into the air when they sense that pests are chomping on their leaves. Insects that are the enemies of pests pick up the signals released from the damaged leaves and they come flying in to the rescue. Many plants release 'attractants' into the air when pests damage their leaves. These attractant molecules attract the enemies of the pest to the plants and soon the saying, 'my enemy's enemy is my friend' pays rich dividends and the plant is pest-free.

Many plants activate a series of chemical signals in their bodies when they sense a pest attack. These in turn, promote the synthesis of toxic chemicals that can act as poisons for the pests that are (or would be) feeding on the plants. The *tomato* plant is a good example of a plant that produces 'signalling molecules' when attacked by chewing insects. The molecules turn on genes that instruct the plant to begin producing certain chemicals that then accumulate in leaves and are consumed by insects. Some plants make powerful steroid-like hormones that interfere with the pest's life cycle, for example by messing up its metamorphosis from the larva to pupa to adult. Biochemist Clarence Ryan and a group of co-workers

Tomato plants can send out chemical SOS messages when faced with a pest attack.

at Washington State University, USA have identified a chemical that plants produce to discourage predatory insects. It gives the insects a bad case of indigestion!

So plants can and do fight back by synthesising toxins that poison attacking insects, or by making repellents that make predators flee. Some plants produce defensive chemicals continually, whether or not they are under attack. Many others only do so in response to an attack.

## So plants can defend themselves, but can they defend their territory?

Territory is perhaps the first thing all living beings need to defend. For only if you are safely settled can you think about making copies of yourself. A large tree that has a huge trunk and a canopy of leaves defends its territory by its sheer girth. It monopolises the available resources because it is taller and has a huge circlet of leaves that catches much of the sunlight. It has deep roots that physically hold the soil together as it ventures deep for water that other plants with shallower roots cannot. Its shade does not allow other plants to flourish. Finally it rules the area it grows on.

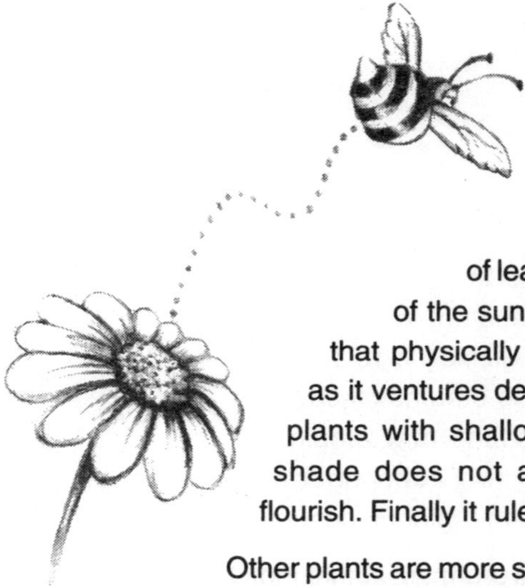

Other plants are more subtle in their approach. When pine needles fall on to the ground, they begin to decompose. The soil absorbs the acid from the decomposing needles. This acid in the soil keeps unwanted plants from growing near the pine tree.

A friend in need is a friend indeed.

Many plants actively release chemicals into the soil to prevent the growth of other plants. This is called 'allelopathy'. The *walnut* tree and *sunflowers* are recognised for using chemicals to prevent other plants from growing too close to them.

A peep into the silent world of plants teaches us many lessons. It demonstrates that the power of friendship is incredible. It shows how by choosing wisely and joining hands with allies and cutting across the species barriers, plants achieve seemingly impossible tasks.

# Read Some More


Andrews, John: *Birds,* Nature Library, Optimum Books, 1993

Attenborough, David: *The Private Life of Plants,* BBC Books, London, 1995

*Nature,* Volume 399, June 1999

*Nature,* Volume 437, September 2005

Rushforth, K.: *Trees,* Nature Library, Optimum Books, 1983

Seymour, Roger S.: 'Plants that Warm Themselves', *Scientific American,* March 1997

H. C. Gangullee, K.D. Dass, C. Datta: *College Botany,* New Central Book Agency, reprinted 2001

# Index

## FLOWERS AND PLANTS

**Acacia**

Also known as thorn tree or wattle.

**Agave**

The most commonly grown species include *Agave americana*, *Agave augustifolia*, blue *Agave* (*Agave tequilana*) and *Agave attenuata.*

**Amorphophallus**

(*Amorphophallus titanium*)

Also called titan arum or voodoo lily.

**Arrow arum**

(*Peltandra virginica*)

Also called virginia wake-robin or tuckahoe.

**Blue delphinium**

Much-admired garden plant.

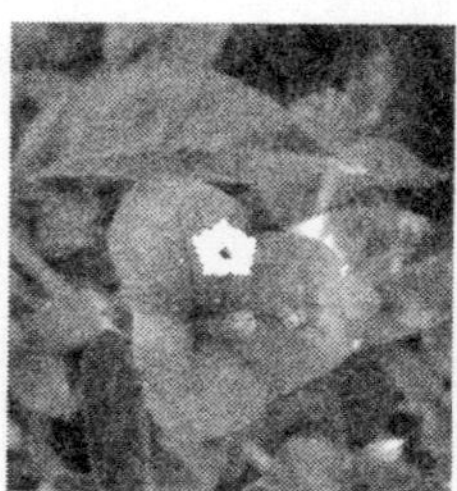

**Bougainvillea**

Named after Admiral Louis de Bougainvillea, who discovered it.

**Cactus**

Any member of the Family Cactaceae.

**Cuckoopint**

(*Arum maculatum*)

Also called lords-and-ladies.

**Dahlia**

National flower of Mexico. Common garden winter annual in India.

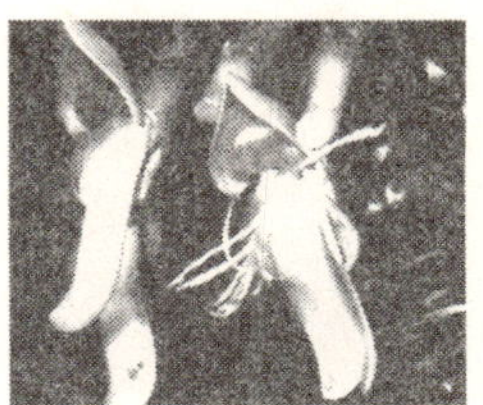

**Deer eye**

(*Macuna holtonii*)

Commonly known as deer eye.

**Foxglove**

(*Digitalis sp.*)

The scientific name means 'finger-like', and refers to the ease with which a flower of *Digitalis purpurea* can be fitted over a human fingertip.

**Helicodiceros**

(*Helicodiceros muscivorus*)

Also known as dead horse arum lily.

**Jasmine**

*(Jasminum sp)*

*Jasminum sambac* is the national flower of Indonesia. In Sanskrit it is called *mallika.*

**Kangaroo paw**

(*Anigozanthos sp*).

Common name for a number of species in the Family Haemodoraceae.

**Lady slipper orchid**

Term used to describe the orchids in the Subfamily Cypripedioidea.

**Lotus**

*(Nelumbo nucifera)*

Also known as Indian lotus, sacred lotus, and sacred water-lily. It is the national flower of India.

**Mexican poppy**

(*Argemone mexicana*)

Also known as argemone, devil's fig, white thistle and prickly poppy.

**Milkweed**

(*Asclepias sp*).

There are different types of milkweeds.

Nicotiana

Also called tobacco plant or flowering tobacco.

Passion vine

(*Passiflora sp*)

Also called passion flower.

*Raat ki Rani*

(*Cestrum nocturnum*)

Also known as night-blooming cestrum, lady of the night, queen of the night, night-blooming jessamine, and night-blooming jasmine.

*Rajnigandha*

(*Polianthes tuberosa*)

Also called tuberose.

Rattan

Rattan (from the Malay *rotan*), is the name for the roughly six hundred species of palm trees that are similar to bamboo.

Saguaro cactus

(*Carnegiea gigantea*)

It is the largest cactus in the USA, commonly reaching a height of 12 metres and an age of up to 200 years.

**Skunk cabbage**

(*Symplocarpus foetidus*)

Also known as eastern skunk cabbage, clumpfoot cabbage, foetid pothos, meadow cabbage, polecat weed or swamp cabbage.

**Snapdragon**

(*Antirrhinum majus*)

The common name is derived from its fancied resemblance to the face of a dragon that opens and closes its mouth, with a snap, when properly squeezed.

**Sunflower**

(*Helianthus annuus*)

What is usually called the flower is actually a head of numerous flowers or florets crowded together.

**Sweet pea**

(*Lathyrus odoratus*)

The seeds of the sweet pea are poisonous and should not be eaten. The flowers come in a variety of colours.

### Tillandsia

The genus *Tillandsia* was named after the Finnish physician and botanist Dr Elias Tillandz (originally Tillander). Different species are known by different names. For example, *Tillandsia usneoides* is called Spanish moss.

### Traveller's tree

(*Ravenala madagascariensis*)
Also known as traveller's palm.

### Trillium

Also known as wake-robin or birthroot. The three leaves below the flower are the plant's only food source and a picked *Trillium* may die if the leaves are removed along with the flower.